A Crabby Book

Let's Play, Crabby!

Jonathan Fenske

ACORN™
SCHOLASTIC INC.

For Coco, who is the best at finding things!

Library of Congress Cataloging-in-Publication Data

Names: Fenske, Jonathan, author.
Title: Let's play, Crabby! / Jonathan Fenske.
Description: First edition. | New York : Acorn/Scholastic Inc., 2019. |
Series: A Crabby book ; 2 | Summary: Crabby is a very grumpy crab, so Plankton tries to find a game that will cheer Crabby up, but Crabby does not want to play Simon Says or hide-and-seek—will a game of tag be more to Crabby's taste?
Identifiers: LCCN 2018035383 | ISBN 9781338281552 (pbk.)
ISBN 9781338281576 (hardcover)

Subjects: LCSH: Crabs—Juvenile fiction. | Plankton—Juvenile fiction. Games—Juvenile fiction. | Play—Juvenile fiction. | Humorous stories. | CYAC: Crabs—Fiction. | Plankton—Fiction. | Games—Fiction. | Play—Fiction. | Humorous stories. | LCGFT: Humorous fiction. | Picture books.
Classification: LCC PZ7.F34843 Le 2019 | DDC (E)—dc23
LC record available at https://lccn.loc.gov/2018035383

10 9 8 7 6 5 4 3 2 1 19 20 21 22 23

Printed in China 62

First edition, August 2019

Edited by Katie Carella
Book design by Maria Mercado

Today is just another day at the beach.

The **wind** in my face.
The **spray** in my eyes.
The **kelp** in my claws.

It is enough to make a crab **crabby**.

SHHH!

GUESS WHO?
Hmmm.

You **sound**
like Plankton.
You **feel**
like Plankton.
You **smell**
like Plankton.
SNIFF
SNIFF
Do you give up?
No,
I do not
give up.

I will give you a hint.
My name starts with "plank."
I know.
And it ends with "ton."
I know.

That is it.
No more hints.
Well?
Well?!
Well?!
POKE
POKE

I KNOW IT IS YOU,
PLANKTON!

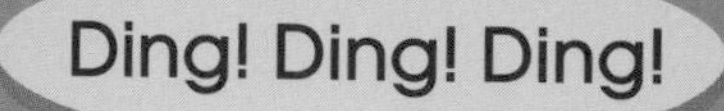
Ding! Ding! Ding!
Plankton is the right answer!

What took you so long?

THE GAME
I **love** to
play games!

Hey, Crabby!
Do you want to
play a game?
No, Plankton!
I do **not** want to
play a game.
I do not like
games.

If you play a game with me, I will be your **best friend**!
I do not need a best friend.
But **everybody** needs a best friend!
Not me.

Yes, you do.
No, I don't.
Yes. You. Do!
Whatever.

So, can we play a game?
Sure, Plankton. We can play a game.
YAY! We can play Simon Says!
Who is Simon?
You can be Simon.

I am not Simon.
I am **Crabby**!
Okay.
I will be
Simon!
YOU are not Simon.
You are **Plankton**!

Fine. We can play
Crabby Says.
That is more like it.

How do you play?

It is easy!

If you say,
"Crabby says,"
I have to do what
Crabby says!

Wait. If I say, “Crabby says,” you have to do what Crabby says?

You got it!

Wow. I think I will like this game!

So, are you ready to play?

Yes!

Really ready?

Yes!

Here we go!

Crabby says—
stop playing
Crabby Says!

THE OTHER GAME
Hey, Crabby.
Do you want to play
hide-and-seek?
No, Plankton.
I do **not** want to play
hide-and-seek.

You can hide.
I will seek.
I do not **want**
to hide.
Okay. I will hide.
You can seek.
I do not **want**
to seek.
We cannot play
hide-and-seek
if you do not
hide **or** seek!
Exactly.

But I **really** want to play hide-and-seek.

Why don't you play hide-and-seek by yourself?

Watch this.

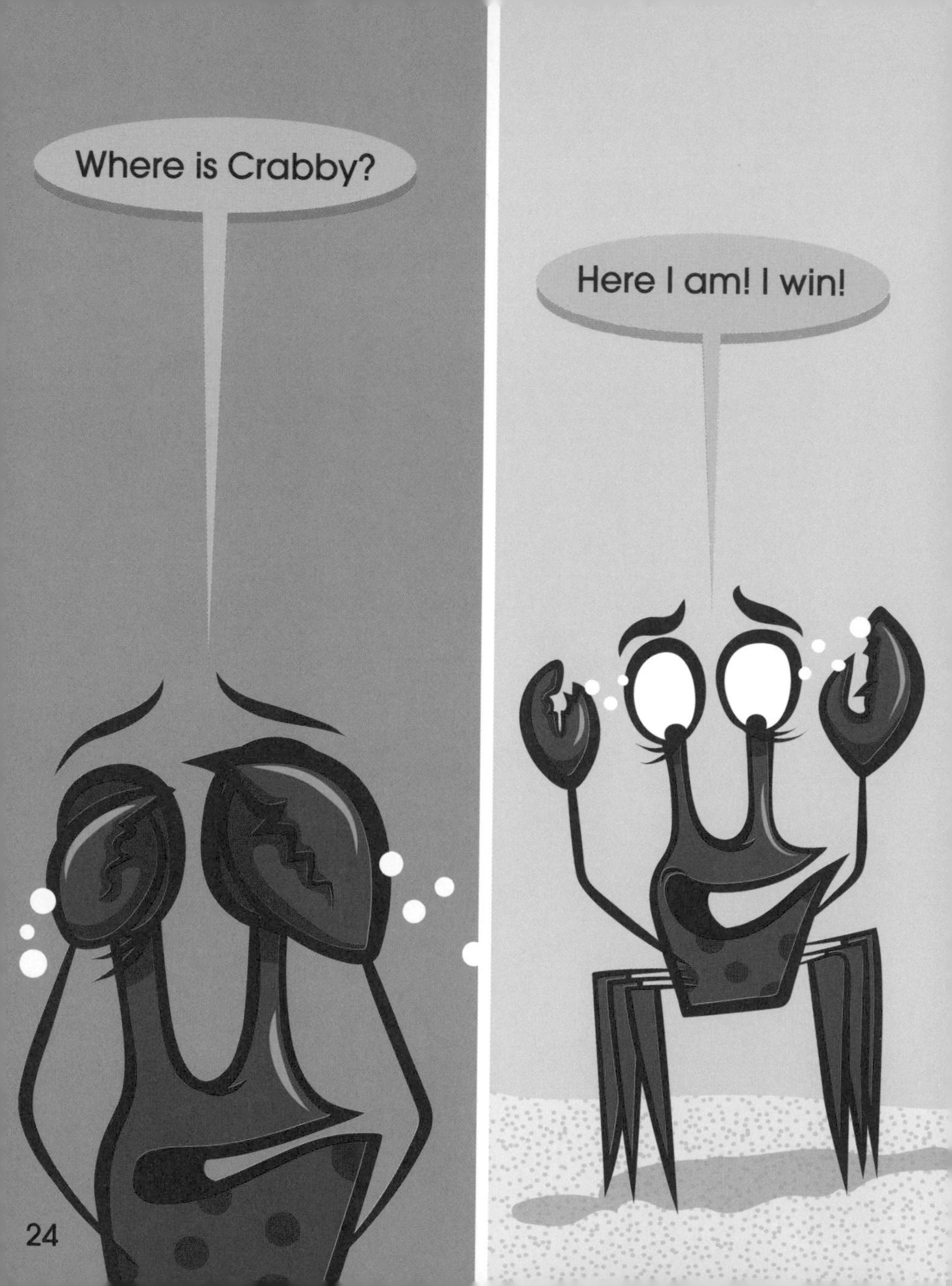
Where is Crabby?
Here I am! I win!

That was no fun.
It was fun for me.
TWITCH
TWITCH

Oh, all right.
One game.

HOORAY!
Can I hide?
Let's flip a coin.

Heads,
I hide.
Tails,
you seek.
Sounds
great!

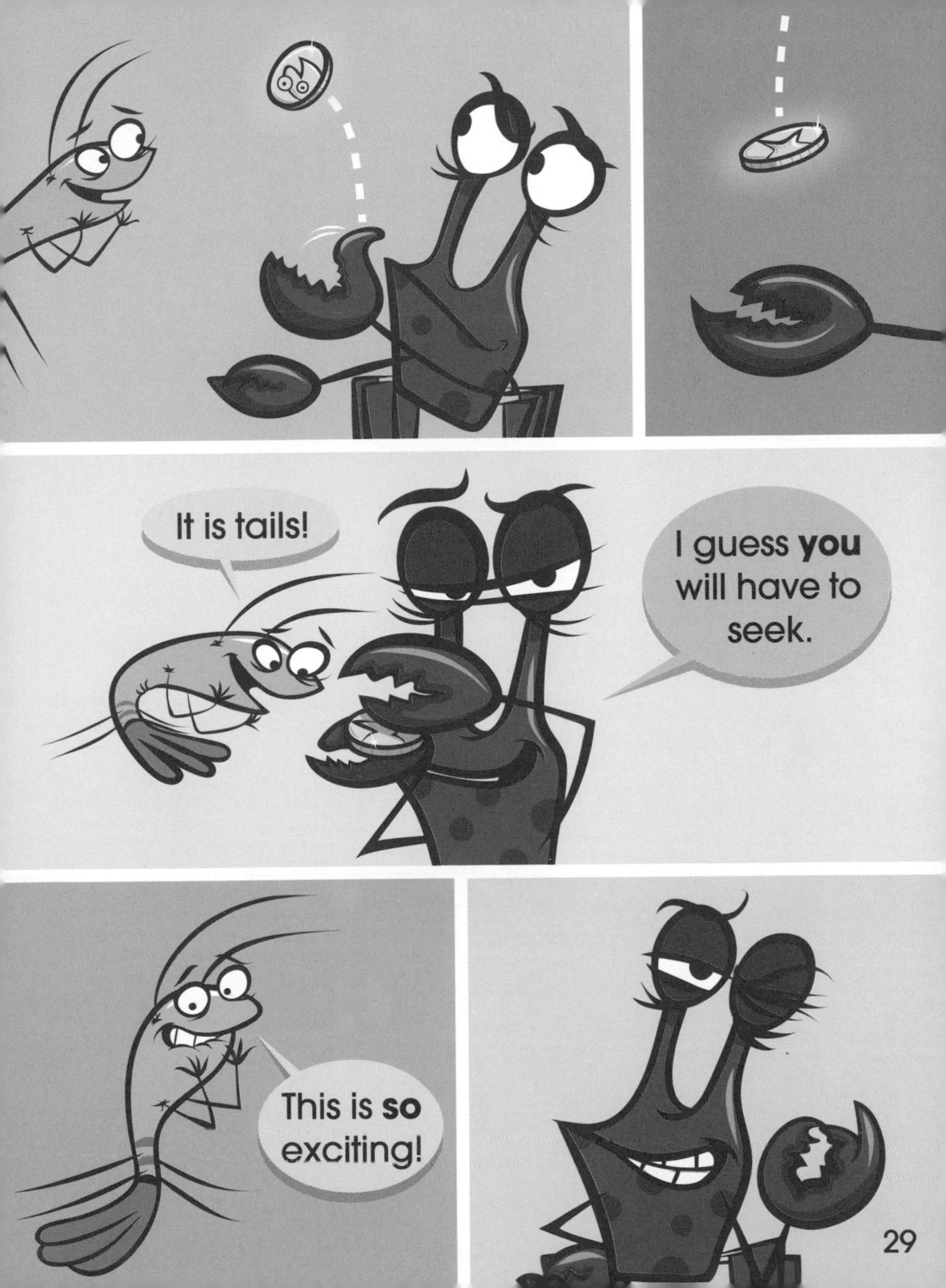
It is tails!
I guess **you** will have to seek.
This is **so** exciting!

I will hide.
I will count
to ten.
It will be **more** fun
if you count to a
thousand.

Okay!
Wait!
A THOUSAND?!
Bye!

377,
378,
379...
SLURP!
Plankton is
PUSHY

THE OTHER
OTHER GAME
Hey, Crabby!
Do you want to
play tag?
No, Plankton.
I do **not** want to
play tag.

Hmmm.
Tag is **more** fun with **more** players.
Hey, Abby, Tabby, and Blabby!
You have **got** to be kidding.

Who wants to play tag?
We do!

NOT IT!

Well, Crabby. It looks like you are **IT**.
Why am **I** IT?
Because you did not say you were **not** IT.
Okay, then. **NOT IT.**
HA!
Sorry!
You are too late!
Hmmm.

What if I
cannot
be IT?
Why can you not be IT?
Shhh.
It is a **secret**.

Oooh!
A **secret**!

Can you tell me?
Nope.
Pleeease?
I **love** secrets!
I love secrets, too.
That is why I **keep** them.

But **best friends** do not keep secrets from each other.
That is true.
Oh, all right. Come here.
Yes!

Closer.
Closer.
Are you ready?
YES!!!
I cannot be IT because—
Tell me! Tell me!

TAG!

Because now **you** are IT!
That's IT, Crabby!

About the Author

Jonathan Fenske lives in South Carolina with his family. He was born in Florida near the ocean, so he knows all about life at the beach! He **loves** to play, and playtime for him is running and climbing mountains.

Jonathan is the author and illustrator of several children's books including **Barnacle Is Bored**, **Plankton Is Pushy** (a Junior Library Guild selection), and the LEGO® picture book **I'm Fun, Too!** His early reader **A Pig, a Fox, and a Box** was a Theodor Seuss Geisel Honor Book.

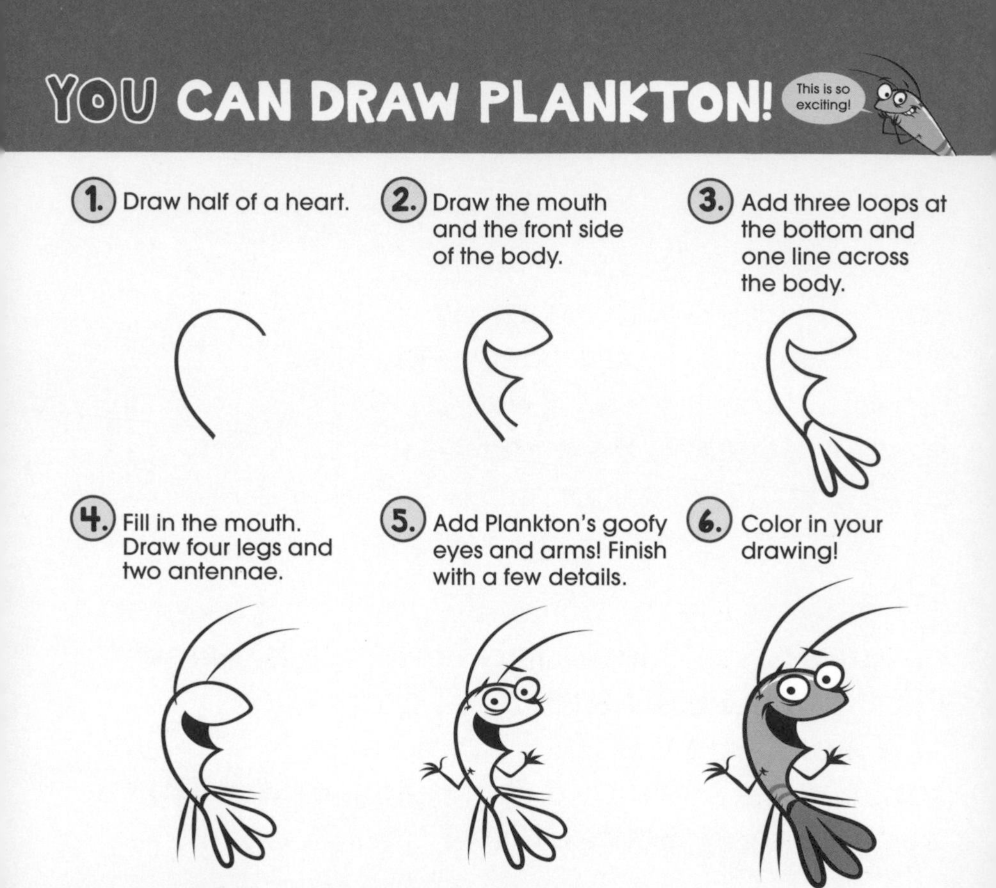

WHAT'S YOUR STORY?

Plankton loves to play games.

What kind of games do **you** like to play?

Would you play games with Plankton?

Would Crabby play with you?

Write and draw your story!

scholastic.com/acorn